Four Winds Chelsea Blue

AN ADVENTURE

Dottie Withrow

by

Dottie Withrow

illustrations by

Robert Brent

Four Winds Chelsea Blue
AN ADVENTURE

Library of Congress Catalog Number: TXu 1-727-972
ISBN-13: 978-0-615-35268-8

Published by Dottie Withrow, Michigan
Illustrations by Robert Brent
Design and layout by Infinity Graphics

For my grandchildren

My name is Chelsea.

My name is on my collar.

My collar has a silver tag.

It has a phone number on it.

Mr. W. brought me home when I was 3 months old.

Mrs. W. gave me my own food bowl.

She gave me healthy treats from the dinner table.

She gave me a cozy bed.

I live with
two bossy cats
named
Princess Anne
and
Daisy Jane.

Princess Anne is very pretty.

She knows she is pretty.

She struts around the house
like the Queen of England.

Princess Anne likes
to tickle me under my chin
with her tail.

I do not like Daisy Jane.

She has sharp, little, white teeth.

She looks like
a Halloween cat.
Daisy Jane likes to
hiss at me to scare me.

I am a very smart puppy.

I am learning to heel, stay, sit,

and come when I am called.

When I meet new people

I put up my paw to shake hands.

One day when Mr. W. went outside

to get the newspaper,

I darted between his knees.

He called,

"Chelsea, come!"

But I did not want to come.

I did not want to
stay in the house.

I wanted to run.

It was a sunny day. The sky was blue.

The air was crisp and cold.

All around were drifts of billowy snow.

What a great day to race and play!

So that is what I did. I ran up and down the street.

I jumped in the drifts of billowy snow.

I played all morning.

I saw my good friend, Boomer Watson.

He was
out enjoying
the day,
too.

Together,
we chased
the squirrels.

We chased the birds.

We chased each other.....

here, there, and everywhere.

We

slipped

and slid

on an

icy pond

like clowns

in a circus.

What fun we had!

Suddenly, the sun

disappeared behind the clouds.

The sky turned gray.

Snowflakes landed on our noses.

Our paws stuck
in the new snow.
We laid down to rest.

Then we looked around.
I did not see my house.
Boomer did not see
his house.

Boomer jumped up
and ran to a house.

He leapt onto the porch.

A man was cleaning
the snow from the steps.

When he saw Boomer, he smiled.

He picked Boomer up

and put Boomer in his rocking chair.

He put a blanket around Boomer.

The man did not see me.

He opened the door and took Boomer inside.

And then he slammed the door.

I wanted to cry!

It is not fun to be alone.

It is not fun to be lost.

It is not fun to be cold.

It is not fun to be hungry.

I wandered and wandered
and wandered.

I wandered all night.

My nose was cold.

I could not sniff the ground

to find a clue for which way to go.

I wanted to be home.

I missed Mr. W. and Mrs. W.

I even missed Princess Anne

and Daisy Jane.

As the sun rose in the morning sky,

the snow sparkled all around me.

I perked up my ears. I opened my eyes very wide.

I looked here, there, and everywhere.

Then I heard a squeak. I saw a gate. As I moved closer,

I noticed a woman walking in her garden.

She was putting birdseed in the feeders.

I did not want to scare the woman.

My paws made no noise.

Slowly and quietly,
I padded
into the garden.

When she saw me,
the woman smiled.

I did all the things
I'd learned.
I wagged my tail.
I sat.
I raised my tired
paw
to shake her hand.

She took
my paw
....and kissed it.

Then she took me
into her house.

She put a blanket
around me.

She fed me
some chicken soup.

I laid down near her fireplace
and went to sleep.

Did I

make it

back

home?

You bet

I did!

That woman was one smart woman.

She saw my name on my collar.

She saw the numbers on my silver tag.

She phoned Mr. W.

When I heard Mr. W.
call "Chelsea, come!",
I gave that woman a slurp
of a kiss on her face....

here, there,
and everywhere.

Then I jumped

into Mr. W.'s car.

Before you could say

"Boomer Watson,"

I was home with Daisy Jane and Princess Anne.

I was home with my own food bowl.

I was home with healthy treats from the dinner table.

I was home with my own cozy bed.

My roaming days are over.

I am not a puppy anymore. I am a big dog now.

I can "heel" when I am out walking.

I will "stay" when I am told to "stay".

I "sit" and "shake hands"

when I am out meeting new friends.

And, when I hear "Chelsea, come!"

I always race to Mr. W's side as fast as I can.

Chelsea's 10
TEACHABLE MOMENTS

TEACHABLE MOMENT 1

The title of the story is Chelsea's full name.
Everyone calls her "Chelsea".
What is your full name?
Do you have a nickname?

TEACHABLE MOMENT 2

Why did Mr. W.
put his phone number
on Chelsea's collar tag?

TEACHABLE MOMENT 3

Chelsea is one of a litter of five puppies.
Mr. W. brought her to his house to live.
How do you think Chelsea feels
coming to live in a new house?

36

Do you think dogs and cats like each other?
What do Princess Anne and Daisy Jane
do to tease Chelsea?
Have you ever been teased?
Who teased you?
Did you like to be teased?

Some dogs have a very keen sense
of hearing, smelling, and seeing.
What tells you that Chelsea has
those keen senses?

Mr. W. is training Chelsea to be a
good dog. Chelsea thinks she is smart
because she knows how to behave.
What do you think
caused Chelsea to misbehave?

Home can be a happy place to be.
Chelsea is happy to be home.
How do you feel when you come back
to your house after you have been away?
Who is there to greet you?

Sometimes a person may let a dog
run outside because they
do not want to walk with their dog.
Is that a good thing to do? Why or why not?
What might happen?

What does a dog do when it "heels"?
Is that a nice way to walk a dog?
How important is it for a dog to "stay"
when he is commanded? How important
is it for a dog to "come" when he is called?
Do you think Chelsea learned an important
lesson when she didn't come?

Have you ever been alone?
When and where were you alone?
Was it scary? Can it sometimes be fun
to play by yourself?

ALWAYS

A Pledge to My Pet

I have chosen you to be my companion…..always.

I will give you a home with a warm bed, healthy food, and fresh water…..always.

I will train you and teach you how to be safe with family and others…..always.

I will provide proper medical care for you…..always.

I will love and respect you…..always.

You will have a collar and tag to identify you if you are ever lost…..always.

I promise that I will be sure that you live in a safe environment…..always.

Pet Name_____

My Name_____

Date_____

Acknowledgements

Many thanks to Dr. Laura Apol, Poet, Author,
and Associate Professor of Children's Literature
in the College of Education at Michigan State University
for her expertise in helping me refine Chelsea's story

and to Robert L. Mahr DVM
for his insight into the world of pet care,
its challenges, and rewards

and to my friend, Susan Stanley.
Her enthusiasm and love of animals
was the inspiration for the "Always" pledge
in the back of this book

About the Author

Dottie Withrow, mother, grandmother,
and retired teacher of children with Special Needs,
wrote Chelsea's story to promote interest in the care
and humane treatment of the animals
we choose to share our lives.
This is her first "Teachable Moments" book.

About the Illustrator

Robert Brent is an artist living in East Lansing, Michigan.
His artistic accomplishments include portraits, murals
and illustrations for books and publications.
Bob thanks his wife Nancy and son Andrew,
and the pets in his life, especially dogs Ozzy and Doris
who posed for illustrations in this book.